By Bonnie Broo
Illustrated by David P

Level Pre Reader

Dalmatian Press, LLC, 2011. All rights reserved.
Published by Dalmatian Press, LLC, 2011. The DALMATIAN PRESS name and logo are trademarks
of Dalmatian Press, LLC, Franklin, Tennessee 37067. No part of this book may be reproduced
or copied in any form without written permission from the copyright owner.

Printed in China

Time to get up, Elmo!
Up, up, up!

The big pup is up.
The pup smells a cupcake.
Yum!

Cookie Monster!
Do not eat up
all the cupcakes!

Ernie is up,
but Bert is not.
Toot-toot-TOOT!
"Stop, Ernie! I give up."

Oh, look!
The baby is up.
The dolly is down.
Down, down, down.

Farmer Grover calls
to six sleepy cows.

"Wake up, cows!
Time for me to milk!"

Oscar pops up.
Bang! Clang! Scram!

Pick up the papers.
One! Two! Three!

Get up, Benny.
The bags must go
up, up, up!

La-la-la!
It is time to wash up!
Scrub-a-dub-dub!

Brush up!
Up and down.

(Not too much!
Do not use it up.)

Bert is up.
What will he put on?
He cannot make up his mind.

Bam! Bam! Bam!

Herry runs up
the street.

All the monsters are up!
All the monsters are out!

Where is Elmo?
Is Elmo up?

Now the monsters are in.
It is time to eat up.

Where is Elmo?
Is Elmo up?

The sun is up.
The birds are up.
And now Elmo is up.
Up, up, up!